Mum and Boy

Stephen Anthony Brotherton

The Book Guild Ltd

First published in Great Britain in 2024 by
The Book Guild Ltd
Unit E2 Airfield Business Park,
Harrison Road, Market Harborough,
Leicestershire. LE16 7UL
Tel: 0116 2792299
www.bookguild.co.uk
Email: info@bookguild.co.uk
Twitter: @bookguild

Copyright © 2024 Stephen Anthony Brotherton

The right of Stephen Anthony Brotherton to be identified as the author of this
work has been asserted by them in accordance with the
Copyright, Design and Patents Act 1988.

All rights reserved. No part of this publication may be
reproduced, transmitted, or stored in a retrieval system, in any form or by any means,
without permission in writing from the publisher, nor be otherwise circulated in
any form of binding or cover other than that in which it is published and without
a similar condition being imposed on the subsequent purchaser.

This work is entirely fictitious and bears no resemblance to any persons living or dead.

Typeset in 12pt Minion Pro

Printed on FSC accredited paper
Printed and bound in Great Britain by 4edge Limited

ISBN 978 1835740 019

British Library Cataloguing in Publication Data.
A catalogue record for this book is available from the British Library.

For Jamie –
I wish I could have been a better dad xx

Contents

Preface	vii
Afterlife	1
Oedipus Revisited	31
Iris May	53
Talking Heads	72
Final Thoughts	85

Preface

Oedipus – a mythical Greek king of Thebes who accidentally fulfils a prophesy by killing his father and marrying his mother. This legend has been cited by philosophers and playwrights throughout the centuries and used by Freud to name his theory of a boy's desire for sexual involvement with his mother whilst holding a sense of rivalry with his father. Extreme examples, but they demonstrate a fascination with the sometimes-complex relationship between mum and son and the unhealthy ways in which this can go badly wrong.

My dad died when I was seven years old, leaving me with just my mum. She was forty-two and never got over his death. I became her little crutch, giving her strength to get out of bed every morning and face the world. I could not have had a better mum. She loved me, cared for me and placed me first at every point in her life. I was, as my sister says, "her blue-eyed boy, who could do no wrong". But that is the point.

How could I possibly live up to that expectation? My formative years set lifelong psychological templates, determining the way I view and interact with the world, especially in relationships. I know these things now, but it's taken years of internal searching and counselling for me to reach this level of awareness. I came through, managed to change, adapt, present myself differently, but it never goes away. It always exists inside my head.

One moment in time, at a vulnerable age, determining everything.

That's what these stories are about. Each of my characters has lessons to learn and to teach. Writing them has been cathartic, but they all beg the same question. How would you react in their place?

Afterlife

My ten-year-old mind matures over decades of afterlife existence, sucking up human learning stored in my DNA. That's how evolution works. I know that now. Nothing is wasted. It's passed from one generation to the next and I've gorged on the database, like a kid in a sweet shop. At Sunday school they gave me a little red book, *The Life of Jesus*, a cover picture of God's son on the cross, winged cherubs floating round his head, beams of sunlight bringing him home. No mention of being trapped in a hole. A new beginning. A fresh start. That's what I need.

I will my toes to stretch for the familiar touch of wood, but all I feel is stiffness gripping my bones and squishy clods of mud squelch underneath my feet. Corpse rot has taken its toll, but I sense the lid above my nose, the sides of oak pushing against my arms, the base underneath my body, separating me from the earth. I try to breathe, but there's nothing, no machinery to push my lungs up and down. Probably for the best – this oxygen dead zone would have me rasping. I wonder why the end of the coffin has disappeared, how the mud has penetrated, how long it will take to swallow up my world. I want to reach behind my head, but rigor mortis, confined space and terror of the unknown hold me back. I'm not ready for the final solution, the ground swallowing me from all sides, but I know it'll take me one day. Earth to earth, dust to dust, my body dissolving into dirt. Maybe I'll move when my bones have gone, become plant fodder, feed a new life. I haven't shifted in what seems like forever, time falling away underground. There's nothing to do but wait. Wait and remember.

That's what I'll do.

Lie in the dark and remember.

*

A smell of cigar smoke wafts through the hallway and chases the closing theme tune of *Minder*. Next up will be the bongs of the *Ten O'Clock News* and a final cup of tea before the house shuts down for the night. Daddy will be puffing on his Hamlet, while Mummy curls up next to him on the settee and sips at a tumbler half-filled with Johnnie Walker.

'He's not right, is he?'

'He'll grow out of it, Joe.'

I adjust my sitting position halfway up the stairs, pull my knees under my chin, fix my eyes on the open lounge door and listen. I want to say something, but I can't force any words. My heartbeat quickens as I press my face against the rails.

'You've been making excuses all his life.'

'There's still time.'

'That gormless look on his face... I wash my hands of him.'

'He tries, love. You know he tries.'

'He's an imbecile.'

'I wish you wouldn't use that word.'

'I've told Rachael to sort him. Poor sod, having him as a kid brother.'

I rock on the stairs and close my eyes. 'Peter,' I whisper. 'Are you there, Peter?'

'What are you doing?'

I look up.

She's hanging over the banister, grinning at me.

'N... n... nothing,' I say.

'You're talking to him.'

'I'm not—'

'He's not real. They'll lock you up.'

'N... n... no.'

'They'll put you in a dungeon, cover you in rats, throw away the key.'

'S... s... stop saying that.'

'There's no point screaming. No one will hear—'

'S… s… shut up. Shut up.'

I ram my hand between my legs, but my stomach lurches and out it comes, a damp warmth soaking my Superman pyjamas. 'S… s… shut up,' I say, rocking myself backwards and forwards.

'Daddy,' shouts Rachael, 'Jake's wet himself again.'

*

A draught snakes up and down my torso, making me shiver. I tell myself to ignore it, concentrate on remembering, try to work out how many years have passed since I last saw the light of day. It's not something you can track in a box, but it doesn't stop my buzzing brain from trying to work it out. Mummy. Daddy. Rachael. My family. They must be dead, lying in a hole like me. Maybe not. Mummy said I was special. Gifted, she called me. I'd draw pale horses for her, wild and galloping through heathers and across moors, their manes pinned back in the wind. 'How do you make them look so real?' she'd say. I'd shrug and draw another. Perhaps we'll meet again. I'd like that. I miss Mummy.

Daddy carried me everywhere when I was a baby. That's what Mummy told me. 'Frightened to put you down in case you hurt yourself.' I wish I could remember. She must have made it up. I waited for him to say something, anything, tried to please him, tried to make him like me, but he stared at me with dead eyes. Rachael looked up imbecile in a dictionary. 'Trust me to get a div,' she said. Fair enough. Back then, my synapses dawdled before connecting with the real world. Dr Dwyer said I needed patience, but Daddy strapped me with his belt, sparking my head clicks to pull me back into a fog, a place of pretend, sometimes good, sometimes not. My fits scared Mummy, especially when I stood on the bed screaming at her to stop dragging me towards the edge of a burning pit. 'No, Mummy. No.' She shushed me down, wiped my face with a flannel, but only when Daddy wasn't there. No one crossed Daddy.

And then he gave me to Rachael. 'Keep it out of my way,' he shouted. Mummy cried and tried to stop him, but Daddy raised his hand and she winced.

'Don't worry, Mummy,' said Rachael. 'I'll look after him.' That made Mummy cry more.

And that's when the games started.

*

Rachael rests her dolls, Jemima and Florence, against the flowerpots on the patio. She looks at me. 'Sit next to them,' she snaps.

'I don't want to,' I say, dropping my head and staring at the floor.

She strides over and slaps my face. 'Do as you're told.'

I bite back tears, hold my stinging cheek and squat next to Jemima.

'Now,' says Rachael, picking up a pink plastic shovel. 'Time for a taste test.'

She walks along the line from Jemima to Florence to me, holding out the shovel, a white ornamental stone resting on its surface. 'Take a lick.'

I stick out my tongue and tip touch the chalky rock.

'I said lick,' says Rachael.

I do it again, this time forcing a swipe, picking up a coating of dust.

'Good,' she says, throwing the stone into a clump of ornamental grasses.

I swallow hard when I see what Rachael picks up off the block paving. 'This time, a bigger lick,' she says, holding the shovel under my nose.

A worm wriggles in front of me.

'Do it,' says Rachael, grabbing my hair and turning my head towards the coal shed, 'or you know what'll happen.'

I lean forward. The worm moves again. 'I… I… I can't.'

'Do you want me to lock you up? Leave you in the dark with spiders the size of mice?'

'N… n… no,' I say.

'You have to do as I tell you. Don't you remember what Daddy said?'

I hesitate, edge closer to the shovel and lick the worm's claggy head, causing it to curl into a ball. I retch and spit on the ground.

'Good,' says Rachael, striding back to the grasses. 'Last taste, but this time you have to chew.'

'Y... y... you can't make me,' I say, looking at the shovel.

'I can do what I want. Eat it.'

Tears streak my cheeks.

She moves the shovel closer.

I pick up a piece of dog turd and put it in my mouth.

*

Something shifts the mud around my feet. I push away the thought of what it might be, but my imagination refuses to switch off. That's the puzzle of this hole. Flesh dissolves to soup, removing all trace of recognisable identity, but my mind continues stretching, learning, cursing me with conscious thought. A bubbling noise as the mud moves again. I wish I could see, but darkness smothers everything. Another puzzle. Seeing without eyes. Hearing without ears. And touch. And smell. Senses intact, but a body long gone.

'Hello, Jake.'

'Peter?'

'Who else?'

A hand touches my arm. 'Where have you been?' I say.

'They wouldn't let me come until now. Have you missed me?'

'Every day. It's scary here.' Arms hug me, lift me into a cuddle. 'That's nice,' I say.

'You always liked being held,' says Peter.

I snuggle in, try to ignore the burrowing noise in the mud, tell myself to enjoy company for the first time since they screwed down the lid. A hand strokes my shin. 'Is that you?' I say.

'Not me,' says Peter, squeezing closer.

I stare up into the dark, think about the depth of soil above me, thud, thud, thudding on the coffin lid when they shovelled in dirt to fill the hole, making me flinch, muffling to nothing, leaving me trapped. My bones ache. It's happened more over the last days, weeks, years. I have no idea how long, but I know my joints feel like they're straining to release the stiffness. It's nice, gives me a memory of everything working, a time of connection. Maybe life is returning, giving me another chance. I cried when the last of my flesh fell, salty tears dripping down my skull and into my mouth. There I go again. Corpses can't taste, or cry. Maybe tears have scarred my bones. I touch my left wrist, find the familiar dent. Dwyer said it would straighten out by itself, but it never did. Maybe it didn't have time.

More bubbling.

'P… P… Peter. Is that you, Peter?'

*

Mummy buys me Famous Five books, brings them to my room when she comes back from Preedy's newsagent's. Daddy won't let me mention Peter now. Mummy set him a place at the dinner table, but Daddy got cross with us whispering to each other and smashed up his chair. We read under the sheets. Peter thinks George and Timmy the dog are best, but I like Anne, the quiet one. She's got all the brains.

Rachael wakes me with a punch on my arm. 'Get up,' she snarls.

I rub my eyes and look at the bedside clock. 'But it's only five—'

She thumps me again. 'Don't argue.'

I turn out of bed, slide Snoopy slippers on my feet. 'I need a wee,' I say.

'No time,' she says, grabbing my hand and dragging me towards the door.

'Where are we going?'

'To have some fun.'

The park is silent apart from a raspy chattering magpie sitting on the top branch of an oak tree. We walk into the playground, Rachael still gripping my hand. She sits me on a swing. 'You see that bar,' she says, pointing upwards. 'I'm going to push you over it.'

My eyes follow her finger to the top of the frame. 'N... no,' I say, going to stand up. 'It's too high.'

'Don't be a baby,' she says, pushing me back on the seat.

I grip the ropes.

'Loop the loop. Over the bar,' she chants, her hands falling harder and harder on my back. 'Loop the loop. Over the bar. Loop the loop. Over the bar.'

Higher. Higher. Higher.

My grip on the rope tightens, breeze drags my face. A harsh ascending screech from the magpie fills the air. Rachael's hands hit my back again. Slide, roundabout, river. They all whoosh past me. My bladder slackens as I fall and grips like a vice as I shoot back up. 'Don't wee. Don't wee.' I bite my lip, squeeze my eyes together. 'S... s... stop,' I scream. 'Stop.'

'Loop the loop. Over the bar. Loop the loop. Over the bar.'

Skywards. Back to earth. Skywards. Back to earth.

Higher, higher, higher.

'S... s... stop. Stop.'

'Oi, you.'

I open my eyes. A man with a walking stick raised in the air strides towards us across the football pitch. 'I can see you,' he shouts.

Rachael grabs the ropes, judders me to a stop. 'Run,' she says.

*

I made Peter on my sixth birthday.

He dropped out of my head the same age as me, with blond hair and deep-set black eyes. He looks scary and he frightened me at first, but he's like a fluffy rabbit who gives world champion cuddles. We played cowboys and Indians, and garages with a wind-up lift and Matchbox cars. I liked tractors best, but Peter preferred dragsters, shooting them across the room like they'd been fired from a catapult.

The stroking hand moves upwards and rests on my knee. 'Who is that?' I say.

'Don't be scared,' says a woman's voice.

'It's okay,' says Peter, hugging me again. 'You're safe.'

'B… but—'

'Don't speak,' says the woman, her hand touching my arm, her breath warming my face. 'It's time for you to leave.'

I hear a click of fingers, feel lips lightly kiss my forehead.

'Relax,' says Peter. 'Let her take you.'

'Take me…' Something grabs the words, hushes me into silence.

Peter's hug loosens and sets me free. New arms encircle me. 'Breathe,' says the woman.

'I'm not—'

'Trust me,' she says.

I try to make out her face, but I can't penetrate the darkness. There's a smell. It reminds me of Mummy's perfume. White musk. 'Breathe,' she says again.

I force myself to try, once, twice.

Another finger click.

*

I walk along the shoreline of a deserted beach, hand in hand with Mummy, licking my ice cream and looking out to sea. A black mass of cloud anchors itself on the horizon. Something bursts from its centre and flies towards us. 'What is it, Mummy?'

'A dragon,' she says.

The creature reaches the beach, hovers above our heads. Its fleshy underbelly and green spiky back scales fit together like intricate jigsaw pieces.

'Dragons aren't real, Mummy.'

'This one is.'

A thud as the dragon lands on the sand, making me drop my cornet. 'Come with me,' it says.

Mummy lets go of my hand, walks over and climbs on its back. 'I have to go,' she says.

'Come back, Mummy,' I shout, but she ignores

me, leans over and whispers something in the dragon's ear. The dragon flies off in the direction of the clouds.

I turn, walk off the beach, down the high street, back towards town. Daddy is in front of me, sitting at a table in the al fresco area of a coffee shop. He's drinking cappuccino and eating a slice of Bakewell tart. Rachael is opposite him with her back to me. They're laughing. Daddy squeezes Rachael's hand.

I walk up the path, stand next to their table. 'Mummy,' I scream. 'Mummy.'

'Imbecile,' says Rachael, turning towards me.

Daddy wipes Rachael's cheek with a serviette, peeling her skin and dropping it with a splat on the table.

'Mummy,' I scream. 'Mummy.'

*

The woman lies against my back and wraps her arms around my body. She lifts me through darkness, splitting the wood and corkscrewing us through the dirt. I break the surface into life, sunlight hitting my face. I gasp, suck, blow, feel my chest rise and fall. A flow of blood warms the chill of death out of my system as muscles and skin roll back over my bones. I look down. We're flying over the cemetery. Below me is my grave, set at the far end of the churchyard, isolated from the other headstones in a carpet of bluebells. 'Are you okay?' whispers the woman.

'Who are you?' I ask.

She hugs me closer.

I look back at the ground. We're circling the graveyard. I stretch my legs, tighten my muscles, tauten my skin, hinge my knees and ankles, bask in the joy of movement. I want to do the same with my hands and fingers, touch my face, my hair, but I'm frightened to let go of the woman's arms. I move my tongue around the inside of my mouth, run it over my lips and then blink my eyelids. For so long, there's been nothing. Darkness and bone. I take a deep breath, look around me. Fields reach out to the horizon, fluffs of clouds roll across an azure sky. More deep breathing. Smells of grass and cow dung, a sound of church bells. I summon up courage, let go of her arm with my right hand and pat my chest. It's odd, like an imposter. My mature brain is reunited with a ten-year-old body. I'm an adult possessing a child – that's how it feels.

'Hold on,' says the woman.

I grip her arm again. We turn and head towards the horizon, the wind flattening my cheeks as she quickens our speed. 'W… w… where are we going?' I say.

'Don't be frightened,' she says.

I see a lake in the distance.

We land each end of a rowing boat without causing a ripple across what turns out to be a milky millpond. Grasses overhang the banks and chirping crickets intensify the silence, making me scared to speak. My mind races. I touch my body. I'm dressed in shorts, white T-shirt and black plimsolls. 'You'll have questions,' says the woman.

I take in her image. Blue pinstripe suit, red pixie boots, spiky blonde hair. Not the Angel Gabriel. 'Who are you?' I say again.

She holds out her hand. 'I'm Mim,' she says.

I shake her hand. It feels strange, a little boy doing something so formal, but my mature brain tells me it's the right thing to do. 'I don't—'

'You've been chosen,' she says.

There's movement in the grasses. A duck honks as it flies out, silencing the crickets for a split second before they start up again. My eyes are watering. I wipe them with the back of my hand.

She reaches over and touches my knee. 'You're still adjusting,' she says. 'You should rest before we move on.'

'What do you mean chosen?'

'For another shot at life. That's what you want, isn't it?'

'But how—'

'You'll see,' she says. 'First, you need sleep.'

*

A full moon lights up the night sky. Rachael drags me through our garden, out the back gate, and we tramp across a playing field. We reach a metal wire fence, and she sits me on the grass in front of her. 'There it is,' she says, pointing. 'The wooden building with the weeds in front of it.'

I look nervously at the petrol can at her feet. 'What is it?' I say.

'The science block, Div. I've told you already.' She reaches in the pocket of her jean shorts, pulls out a box of matches and shakes them in my face. 'And you're going to set it on fire,' she says.

I look again at the building, click my head into a dream, take the matches and pick up the can. 'Do as she says. Do as she says.' It's like I'm outside of my body, watching it all unfold on a screen. 'It isn't me. It isn't me.'

Rachael stands, places her hands on my shoulder and turns me towards her. 'You're not going to let me down, Jake?'

'N… no,' I say, wincing as she pinches my arms.

'Good lad. And you know what to do with the petrol?'

'Pour it on the weeds and light it.'

'That's right. I'll teach that bastard for putting me in detention.' She pulls me to my feet and pushes me towards the fence. 'I'll hold it up while you slide underneath.'

I race across the field, gripping the petrol can, liquid sloshing with every stride, the hood of my anorak over my head. I concentrate, ultra-conscious of not tripping over, think about Mummy and what she would say. Nothing. Daddy giving me to Rachael means Mummy disowns me as well. The only time we're able to speak is when we're alone. She has shiny, black hair that reaches her waist when I brush it out with her pink-handle hairbrush. Afterwards, I spray her perfume, which sticks to my clothes for days. I yearn for Mummy squeezing me close, the smell of Pledge and Fairy liquid on her working day apron.

The science block comes up on me sooner than I expect. I put the can on the ground and look back. My stomach turns as I realise Rachael is staring at me with her cold eyes through the wire mesh, her arms folded across her chest. I hurriedly unscrew the cap and walk up and down, pouring petrol over the weeds at the base of the building. A sweet smell hits my nostrils, almost like the sticks of liquorice Mummy buys me when Daddy's not around. I sniff my coat, which still has a tinge of Mummy's white musk scent. 'It isn't me. It isn't me.'

I tip the can, pour out the dregs and strike a match.
'Run. Run. Run.'

Rachael bellows across the field. It's easier sprinting

without the petrol can, but my feet are slipping on the damp grass. A crackle and pop of weeds tells me the match has caught. The fuel ignites with a whoosh, acts like a starting pistol, makes me bolt faster towards the fence. I'm panting hard. My head throbs; my face flushes; my heart bangs out of my chest. I want to werewolf scream at the moon. 'It isn't me. It isn't me.'

'Run. Run. Run.'

I'm nearly there. Rachael crouches down, hands on top of her head. She screams at me, but her eyes are fixed on the fire. A bang, and then the sound of splintering wood. Rachael covers her mouth.

I reach the fence, skid underneath.

She hugs me. 'Jesus, Jake. Look what you did.'

We stand side by side and stare at the science block inferno.

I burst into tears.

*

I can't take my eyes off the milky lake and azure sky; stop sucking in the scents of eucalyptus and rhododendron flowers drifting across the water; give up being entranced by the background hum of chirping crickets. A waft of breeze tickles my face. I wonder what's happened to Peter, but I'm not worried. He'll come back when he can.

I rub my thighs. It feels nice. My flesh is fully

restored and fired for life. Mim is cross-legged at the opposite end of the boat with her eyes shut. Something tells me to tiptoe through until she wakes up. I turn inwards, let my mind somersault thought after thought, try to process what has happened, and what's about to happen. Another shot. That's exactly what I want, but why now after so long?

Mim opens her eyes and smiles. 'It's not complicated,' she says. 'You had to wait for your time.'

'I don't understand.'

'Do you remember what happened?'

'Sort of.'

'We couldn't just ignore it.'

'But I was a little boy.'

She reaches inside the jacket of her pinstripe suit and pulls out a packet of More menthol cigarettes and a Clipper lighter. She lights up and takes a long drag, blowing smoke across the lake. 'You're not a little boy now,' she says.

I look down at my shorts and plimsolls.

'That's just clothes,' she says.

'I feel different,' I say. 'More alive.'

'You've been learning?'

'My brain has sponged everything.'

'We wanted you to feel loved. You didn't deserve what happened to you.'

A splat of rain lands on the back of my neck, followed by another.

'We need to move,' says Mim, grabbing the oars and starting to row.

'Where are we going?'

'You'll see,' she says. 'Just be patient.'

*

Mummy lies in her room most days. Her "turns" she calls them. She never has them in the evening when Daddy's there, back from the bank. Daddy likes her with him, cooking his tea, watching telly, drinking whisky. Some days, she lets me stay at home and I cuddle next to her. She hums Jim Reeves songs, like "Bimbo", and, if she's feeling well, we play Snakes and Ladders. Other days, she puts make-up on me, pink powder puffing my cheeks, a splash of red lipstick round my mouth, a stroke of mascara to thicken my lashes. 'Wash it off,' she says, 'before your father and sister get home.' I leave it on until the last minute, but today I fell asleep on the bed next to her, dreaming about swimming with pods of dolphins, nuzzling me as they glide through the tide.

'What's that crap on your face?' yells Daddy, shaking me awake.

Mummy wakes up as well and jumps to her feet. 'Leave him, love,' she says. 'It's my fault.'

'It's not enough him being an imbecile,' says Daddy. 'You're turning him into a pansy.' He grabs me by the scruff of my T-shirt and throws me off the bed.

I land with a thump on the carpet and scuttle into a corner, knees up against my chest, tears welling in my eyes. *Don't cry. Don't cry.* My arm hurts from the bang against the floor. I start to hum and rock backwards and forwards.

'Leave him alone,' screams Mummy, grabbing Daddy's arm.

He slaps her face, and she falls back on the bed. 'He's got to learn,' he says, slapping her again.

I lift my head. Mummy crawls across the duvet, but Daddy grabs her feet, pulls her back towards him, punches the mattress. A shiver goes through my body. I run my hand over my face, smearing snot and tears across my cheeks. 'You've ruined him,' spits Daddy into Mummy's eyes.

I jump up, race over and kick Daddy's leg. 'L... l... leave her alone,' I scream. 'L... l... leave her alone.'

Daddy turns, his eyes on stalks. 'You little shit,' he says, crashing the back of his hand against the side of my head.

I hit the floor again, my arm crunching underneath me.

'I'll take him, Daddy.'

I look towards the bedroom door. Rachael grins, walks over and pulls me to my feet.

'Get him out of my sight,' says Daddy.

'Don't hurt him,' says Mummy.

Daddy steps towards her and she cowers. 'She'll do what she wants,' he says. 'It might knock some bloody sense into him.'

*

Thick darkness smothers the coal shed, giving me nowhere to focus but inside my head. It feels like I've been in here for hours, twitching at every prickle on my skin, waiting for spiders and God knows what else to race over my body. I lick my dry lips, try to taste a trace of sticky lipstick, but there's no moisture in my mouth. My stomach aches and I'm worried about my left wrist, which is swollen and throbbing, my arm hanging limp at my side. In my mind, I run along the beach with Tina, our Staffordshire bull terrier. We've had her from a puppy and Mummy says they bought her when I was born, which means Tina's ten. The hair around her mouth has turned grey, and she gets locked in here sometimes. She nuzzles me when I stroke her, but I don't know where she is now. I can smell her in the coal shed. It makes me cough.

A click in the padlock on the shed door. It swings open. Rachael stands with her back to the night sky, looking at me. She flashes a torch, shining it directly in my face. 'What's that smell?' she says, shifting the beam around the shed floor. She stops at a pile of coal in the corner. 'Oh,' she says. 'Couldn't you have waited?'

My cheeks flush and I drop my head.

'You'll have to clean it up later,' she says. 'Come on.'

'Where are we going?'

'Daddy wants me to teach you a lesson.'

'B… b… but I've been in here for hours.'

'What's the matter with your arm?'

I turn away from her. 'Nothing,' I say.

She grabs me, twists my body to face her and yanks my arm in the air.

I scream.

'Jesus,' she says, letting go of me. 'You've broken it.'

I slump back on the coals.

'Does it hurt?' she says, standing over me.

'Y… y… yes.'

She stamps on my wrist.

*

Mim manoeuvres the boat alongside a wooden jetty. 'Throw me the rope,' she says, jumping out and holding her hand towards me.

I throw as hard as I can, just about reaching the boards in front of her feet.

She grabs hold before it slides over the edge and

into the water and secures it with a granny knot around a mooring post. 'Come on,' she says. 'We have some walking to do.'

'Where are we going?'

She ignores me and strides off into the forest in front of us.

I trundle after her, birdsong filling my ears. I want to ask again, but something tells me it would be pointless. 'Keep calm,' I tell myself. 'You'll find out soon enough.' My mind shifts into top gear, tries to calculate what the answer might be. The possibilities are limited, given that I'm dead. Sunday school lessons come flooding back. Heaven versus hell. Mim said another shot, that I'd had to wait my time, what I'd done couldn't be ignored. But surely being buried for decades had repaid any debt. The years and years of lying in limbo must count for something. Buddhism's rebirth. That's it. They were sending me back.

We walk uphill, sunlight streaking through canopies and spotting our progress. A memory of the grave makes me suck in fresh, clean air, blow away the claustrophobia of the hole, the dirt above me, being trapped in rotting wood. I check out all my movements, make sure everything is connected. Wriggling toes as my feet land on the earth, stretching hands as I bat away branches to clear my path, bending knees and elbows. My flesh feels warm, pins and needles pushed away as new blood flows and reaches the extremities. Every single heartbeat, eye blink and nostril sniff register. I tongue roll my mouth and then drool over my lips to moisten. I have to stop when exertion overwhelms me, panting myself back under control, lifting the bottom of my T-shirt to wipe beads of sweat off my brow. I keep my eyes on Mim's back. If she goes too far out of sight, I panic and run to catch up, tripping over stray roots and brambles in the process. A couple of times I fall, grazing my knees.

Mim keeps the same steady pace, not once checking if I'm okay, and then, at the top of a hill, standing in a clearing, she comes to a halt and faces me. 'We're here,' she says. 'This is where it begins.'

*

The skin under my Plaster of Paris is itching. It feels like a nest of ants are nipping at me, trying to get through the layers to suck at my blood. Mummy gave me one of her knitting needles to scratch it, but no matter how hard I try, there's always a spot close to my hand that I can't reach properly. At least I can move my fingers now, and the pain has dropped to a dull ache. Daddy told the hospital I'd fallen over playing football, been slide-tackled by the cock of the school. The male nurse ruffled my hair, said it would heal quickly at my age and all lads needed a war wound.

Daddy laughed and glared at me. The itch is getting worse. I want to rip the cast and gouge the skin.

'What are you going to do?' says Peter.

I shrug and stare out over the playing fields. Some of the kids from school are playing football on one of the pitches, two sides kicking into one goal. Cooper, a greasy-haired lad who lives on our street, shouts "spacka" at me when he runs my way to fetch the ball. I need to go soon before they finish their game. Giving me a kicking on their way home would make their day. Peter puts his arm around me. I lean closer to him, and he squeezes my shoulder.

Our house has fallen into a sulky silence. Daddy walks around with a thundercloud over his head, and him and Rachael look straight through me, as though I'm a ghost. He watches and checks everything since he caught me covered in make-up. I hear Mummy sobbing in her bedroom, which makes me sad. Daddy fetched her a bag of tablets from the chemist, but it doesn't seem to have made any difference. The bruising around her eye has gone down, but it's still puffed from Daddy's slap after slap after slap. Rachael grabbed my face and said she'd lock me up again if I said anything.

One of the lads on the pitch shouts "goal" and runs around punching the air. Three of the other boys jump on him, wrestle him to the ground in celebration. The goalie picks the ball from the back of the net and kicks it out of his hands to restart the game. They're all wearing their favourite football shirts. I look down at my muddy pumps and grazed knees. My cast is a dirty off-white. Hobbs, a fifteen-year-old Led Zep fan who lives next door to us, broke his leg and everyone signed his plaster, especially the girls. He kept it as a souvenir, stood it in his bedroom. Another shout from the pitch. Two boys are face to face; one of them shoves the other; a couple of other lads run over and pull them apart.

An image of Mummy's swollen eyes drops into my head, Daddy standing over her with his fist raised, Rachael grinning in the doorway. 'I want to kill them,' I say.

'I know,' says Peter. 'I know.'

The red digits on the clock at the side of my bed tell me it's 5am.

I throw back the sheet and blanket, drop my feet to the floor and pad onto the landing. My arm is aching and itching. I stand still for a second, close my eyes and make my head click to shut out everything except my thoughts. 'It isn't me. It isn't me.' I feel sorry for Mummy, but it's probably for the best, and I can't think of a way of doing this without including her. Peter came up with the idea, reminded me of a show Mummy and Daddy had watched. We'd listened to it from the stairs. *Play for Today*. That's what it was called. Anyway, it's the same as Rachael made me do to the science block and that seemed to work okay.

I open my eyes. No lights. I cross the landing, down the stairs. My head click gives everything a watery vision. It's like I'm on autopilot, almost zombie-like. The walking dead. Bravo, from school, told me about them. It made me want to sit in the cemetery at night, just to see if any of the bodies cracked the surface of their grave and came back to life. I never did. Peter said it wasn't a good idea.

Down the hall. Into the kitchen. Mummy's box of long matches sit on the walnut worksurface in front of me. 'I need a new cooker,' Mummy would say to Daddy. 'One that lights itself.'

'That'll see you out,' Daddy would snarl back.

'Are you sure this is what you want?' says Peter.

I turn the plates and oven knobs on. Gas hisses as it releases into the air. There's no smell, which surprises me.

We slouch against the cooker side by side. I look at the wall clock. Fifteen minutes before the central heating fires. That should be enough.

Peter nods and we hug.

*

Night falls.

Mim has led us down the hillside and we're standing next to a rippling lake, a full moon reflecting off its surface, legions of pond hoppers skating across fresh green lily palms and a swarm of mosquitoes hovering at the reedy banks. A blanket of mist drops, shrouding the water in ribbons of fog, which chase each other like a posse of ghosts in an elaborate game of twister.

Peter squeezes my hand, and we smile at each other. A whisper of wind clears the air. Sitting cross-legged in front of us are a row of four smoke humans. Eyes, nose, mouth, all fading in and out of existence. They hum, shifting up through the vocal ranges, bass, baritone, tenor, hitting soprano, throwing their hands skywards, their black eyes staring expectantly towards the heavens.

'Lost souls waiting for a new life,' says Mim.

'What are they doing?'

'Calling to God. Maybe one day He'll hear them.'

We walk through a fig orchard. I keep my eyes fixed on the floor, weaving a careful path through clumps of stinging nettles, conscious of my bare legs. 'How much further?' I say, wiping sweat from my face.

'We've arrived,' she says, pointing towards a lush lawn with a eucalyptus tree in its centre.

I stare into its branches.

'A reunion tree,' says Peter.

'We need the dust arrangers,' says Mim.

She claps three times. The dirt at the foot of the tree swirls faster and faster, mashing through the grass, circling, making its way up the trunk, floating higher and higher, disappearing into the eucalyptus. She claps again. A prism of white light drops from the tree's canopy.

A smiling face. Shiny black hair reaching her waist.

'Mummy,' I say.

Mim touches my shoulder. 'Climb, Jake,' she says. 'Your new life is waiting for you.'

Oedipus Revisited

At twelve years old I married Mum.

Her eyes filled with tears when I asked her, and she baked a Victoria sponge to celebrate. 'You're so sweet, Charlie.'

We said proper words to each other, which I copied from a book I'd borrowed from the local library. I pushed one of Granny's old dress rings on the third finger of her left hand. It fitted perfectly, which we knew it would because Mum wore the ring every so often when she went to bingo. We watched telly afterwards, an old black-and-white film, *Breakfast at Tiffany's*, starring Audrey Hepburn. 'What a perfect day,' Mum said and kissed me on the cheek before we went up to bed.

We never told anyone, but that didn't make it less real, and we carried on living as before. Mum had reached her half-century by that time, but she still had a slim figure and doe-like brown eyes framed by thick lashes and seductive freckles across the bridge of her nose. Her naturally tanned skin, a gene present from a Maltese grandfather, meant she didn't have to wear much make-up, but she wore some, which added to her glamour.

I don't regret what we did. Marrying Mum is the best thing that's ever happened to me.

*

The first time I saw Dad his clothes shouted weirdo, which I liked.

I'd walked into town to get some fresh air, dodging the pavement cracks, taking a break from revising for my O level mock exams, and stopped off to buy a can of Pepsi from the newsagent's. As I came out of the shop, a bloke, clearly on a mission, strode past me through the green entrance gates of the park, nearly knocking me into the gutter. He wore a black trench coat, which flapped around his ankles, pinstripe trousers, red Doc Marten boots and a green beret. He stopped at one of the wooden benches, sat down and placed his Dunlop golfing umbrella at his side.

I was about to head for home when I noticed he'd stood up again and raised his hand in greeting. A woman came into view from the opposite side of the park, walking towards him and waving back. He left his umbrella hooked on the arm of the bench, met her halfway and they hugged and then kissed, a thirty-second kiss on the lips. The man touched her cheek, looked into her eyes and said something. She nodded; they held hands, strolled back to the bench, sat down, still talking, still smiling, still laughing.

I nipped down a side street, leaned against a wall and watched them. The woman holding his hand was my mum, and I thought she was at bingo.

My head screamed, *what the fuck?* I wanted to march over and give him a kicking, but instead I put the can on the floor, closed my eyes and sucked in some deep breaths. This is something Mo, my counsellor, taught me. 'It'll help you control your temper, Charlie.' And it works, most of the time, takes me out of my head for a while. I haven't smashed my fist in anyone's face for months now, but that could be down to an increase in my medication.

Deep breathing over, I opened my eyes. They were still there. Kissing, holding hands. Mum with a man. She'd never needed a man.

For as long as I can remember, it has always been me and Mum. Whenever I'd ask about Dad, she'd call him a waster, some army bloke she'd met in a pub, seen for a couple of weeks and then, without a word, he'd buggered off out of her life. 'People pay a fortune for good quality sperm,' she said, 'and that's all he was good for.' No dad. No men. That's it. 'What do I need a man for, Charlie, when I've got my baby boy?'

I never really thought about it much after that. She never seemed bothered, and we got on with life. Just the two of us. The perfect odd couple.

And then I saw her with the bloke in the park. I didn't know he was my dad then. I only found that out later. Too late as it turned out.

*

Let me tell you about me and Mum.

In 1973, when I was ten years old, the country went on a three-day week. Mum placed her emergency candles around the lounge. 'Bloody strikes,' she said. 'Put some coal on the fire, son.'

I jumped off the settee and walked over to the bucket at the side of the hearth.

'Not too much.'

'I know, Mum. Two big lumps at the back and little ones at the front.'

She sang her way around the room, striking matches on a Swan Vesta box and igniting the braided cotton wicks. It reminded me of Uncle Arthur lighting his pipe, holding a match to his Old Holborn tobacco and puff, puff, puffing away, the veins on his forearms throbbing out through his anchor tattoos. She reached our oak-veneered sideboard and lit a candle next to her highly prized pink dish, with a dancing nymph statue as its centrepiece. The dish belonged to Granddad, and every time she polished it, she threatened to haunt me if I didn't look after it when she'd gone.

She caught me looking at her and smiled. 'You're a good boy,' she said.

I flopped on the carpet in front of the fire, listened to the slack as it crackled away and watched the yellow and blue flames pull up the chimney. My cheeks felt flush and toasty. Mum's porcelain dogs looked down on me from the mantelpiece.

She put her matches away in the sideboard drawer and sat on the floor, cuddling me and touching my face. 'You okay, Charlie? You warm enough?'

I nodded.

'Brush my hair,' she said, holding out a blue-handle hairbrush.

I knelt behind her, and she pulled out her tightly pinned clips. She shook her head, letting jet-black hair tumble down her back. I brushed. 'That's nice,' she said. 'I've made a steak and kidney pie for tea. We can watch that John Wayne film.'

'Okay, Mum,' I said, still brushing her hair, which became shinier and shinier with every stroke.

*

You see. That's how we spent our lives. Me and Mum. I never needed anyone, and neither did she. We had each other.

It brought me trouble in the real world, but I sorted it. That's what Mo doesn't get. Sometimes a good kicking is the answer; otherwise people take the piss. That's how I've survived. My coping mechanism. It festers inside me like a caged beast, lies dormant, waiting to erupt. And then, boom. My head clicks and out it struts. I'm not sure where it comes from, but I'm glad it's there.

Like this time when I was seven years old. I ran across the damp grass and crossed the ball to Jack. He headed it to one of the kids from the next estate who toe-punted it past the goalie. We jumped on the scorer and hugged him.

Cooper, who lived three doors away from me, fetched the ball from Mr Perry's hedge. 'It's burst,' he said. 'Where'd you get it? It's crap.'

'Mum got it from the market.'

'Tell her to get us another one.' He pushed me in the chest. 'Tell her now. Go on. Go now.'

'I'll ask her tonight,' I said, feeling my head start to boil.

'He's a mummy's boy,' said Cooper, facing the other lads and clapping.

A chant started. 'Mummy's boy. Mummy's boy.'

He pushed me again and they circled me, shoving me backwards and forwards, wide eyes, stupid grins. Someone elbowed me from behind. I swung round and threw a punch. It missed. Cooper laughed. I crashed my fist into his nose. He fell to the floor, and I stomped on his chest. 'You bastard,' I screamed. 'You bastard.'

Everyone stepped back.

Cooper coughed blood onto the grass, and I kicked him in the head. He groaned and I kicked him again.

'Charlie,' said Jack, grabbing my arm.

'You want some,' I said, facing him.

He backed off.

'Never mention her name again,' I said, kicking Cooper one last time in the ribs before picking up the ball and running home.

And they never did. They didn't speak to me either, but that was okay. It brought me and Mum closer. Us against the world.

*

The man and Mum were still sitting on the bench chatting, which I could just about keep a lid on, but every so often he kissed her, making my head click, and then he put his hand on her knee and stroked her thigh. She wore a tarty denim miniskirt that I'd not seen before. How had that happened? She liked me vetting her clothes, always did. 'Does this look okay on me, Charlie?' But not this one. She must have bought it for him.

I spat on the ground, squatted with my back to the wall, snapped the ring pull on the Pepsi and chugged. What else has she been buying? Make-up, perfume. Have they… I didn't want to think about it, tried to push it from my mind, but it loomed over me. How long has this been going on?

A bus pulled up at the stop in front of the newsagent's, blocking my view of the bench. A couple of pigeons *woo-wooed* behind me. I gasped for breath. My head filled with mist. In through the nose. Out through the mouth.

Mum and a man. I'm still calling him man. That's important for you to realise. I don't know he's my dad yet. Do you understand? I don't want you to think I'm an animal.

*

I've always liked choosing her clothes. Ever since I can remember, she's taken me to the shops, into the changing rooms, her parading up and down in high heels, lifting her dress so I could see the new shoes properly. Sometimes the assistants gave us funny looks, but we were used to that. My favourites were the shorts and tops she wore for bed. She had them in every colour and put on a different one according to her mood. Bright yellow suited her best and it meant she'd had a good day. She'd lie on her stomach and get me to massage her calves and the back of her thighs. Long strokes were best.

She has lovely legs, not a blemish on her skin.

'You've got strong hands, Charlie. For a little boy.'

She hasn't asked me to do that for a while, something I should have noticed.

The bus pulled away from the kerb. The man still had his hand rested on her thigh. I placed a bet with myself that he was her new masseur. Sweat beads popped on my brow.

I've just realised Mum's age when she met Dad again. Having me at the end of her thirties would have been a last shake of the bag. She always said I was her little miracle, and that's how she treated me. When we were alone, she called me "Mummy's Little Hubby" and kissed Granny's ring. 'I'll never have another, Charlie.' It made me want to burst. I wonder where Dad appeared from after all those years, materialising out of nowhere like a ghost. Maybe he'd left the army, tracked her down for old times' sake. She never said if he knew about me. And what were the weird clothes about? I can't ask him any of this now, and Mum… well, she's not really talking to me these days. I'm hoping she'll visit, but she needs time. I get that.

*

It started to rain, and that's when they put up their umbrellas, stood up, kissed a goodbye kiss and walked their separate ways out of the park. Mum went out of my sight, but the man came past me, going back in the direction he'd appeared from.

I slugged off the dregs of coke, crunched the can and lobbed it in the wastebin. Following him hadn't been a conscious decision. It happened instinctively, without even knowing why and what for. Looking back, I'd have been better off going home, asking Mum about it, demanding an explanation. But there was nothing logical in my brain at that point. All I could see was his hand on her thigh, his lips sucking her mouth.

And so, I stalked him. Ducking in and out of shop doorways, like a spook.

*

I followed him through the rain-stained streets. He set off at quite a pace, and I'd have lost him in the crowded high street if it hadn't been for his green Dunlop golfing umbrella, showing him out like a beacon. The rain wasn't that bad, only spotting, but he kept the brolly up, maybe as a comfort thing. A couple of puddles had pooled in the road ahead of me, and I moved closer to the shops to reduce the risk of being splashed by cars. The pavement was getting damp, making it difficult for me to see and avoid the cracks. 'Tread on a crack and you'll break your back.' A mantra from my junior school that turned into one of my obsessions. Everyone has them. You just need to pay attention. Mum used to rattle the door off its hinges to check it was properly locked before dragging herself away from the house.

I noticed people staring at the man as he walked past. The green beret probably, but the red Doc Martens added to his oddness. I had him pegged as an artist of some sort. Perhaps a writer. I felt the need to stop and people-watch. Me and Mum liked that. Sitting in the middle of town, watching boring suburbia rush by, the streets mostly filled with joyless no-brains going nowhere. One day, we spotted a couple of geriatrics, man and woman, dressed in full biking leathers, the man with the logo of a Hells Angel chapter on the back of his bomber jacket. They were holding hands and stole the occasional kiss. Mum said they probably had Harley-Davidsons waiting for them in the car park. It filled my head with a dreamy tale, which is what Mum always did.

Like this time. Bonfire night.

Me, six years old, and we were sword fighting with two sparklers, mixing our flashes in, out, in, out, giggling with excitement, until Mum grabbed my hand and pulled me down on the lawn. We lay in our fur-lined-hood parkas, staring up at a full moon and star-filled sky, watching next door's rockets zoom towards the heavens. A shooting star crossed our vision, and Mum put her hand on my chest. 'You see it, Charlie. You know what that means.'

I shook my head and looked at her.

'We'll be together forever. Just you and me.' She rolled over and kissed the tip of my nose. 'Come on, I'll get those jacket potatoes out of the oven.'

*

The crowds along the high street thickened, which made the man slow down. I feel the need to keep reminding you, I didn't know he was Dad, and there was nothing about the way he looked that screamed ex-army. In fact, as I jogged behind him, I wondered where Mum could have met such a weird creature, but then the thought of Mum meeting a man of any sort was so far off my radar, none of it computed. Maybe she'd signed up with one of those dating agencies. A desperate women of a certain age, grasping at an offer of being wanted, being held. It reminded me of a film me and Mum watched, *Brief Encounter*, which was all about a chance meeting at a railway station. A bored housewife in a dull marriage, falling for a man who removed a piece of grit from her eye. But that ended with decency and honour, not stroking a woman's bare thigh on a park bench. In any case, Mum wasn't bored or desperate. She was happy. We were happy. Perhaps she wasn't. Maybe it was all a sham. No. That couldn't be right. It was his fault. This weirdo had seduced her, turned her away from me. He probably did it all the time, had a string of women he'd speared to his mattress before racing away.

The rain dried up and he stopped in a shop doorway to put his umbrella down. I came to a halt next to a jeweller's, rammed my hands in the pockets of my jeans and clenched my fists. The woman in the shop came from behind the counter, stood in the doorway and smiled at me.

I saw the man set off again, his brolly now folded. My skin prickled at the thought of him grunting and groaning on top of Mum. I made up my mind and sealed his fate. That's when my tracking turned into a chase.

*

Last Christmas me and Mum had our first dance.

We dragged a seven-foot tree through the slush of melted snow and back to our house. She opened the front door. 'It's huge,' she said. 'Where are we going to put it?'

'Let's put it in the front room.'

'It's too big. Let's set it up in the dining room by the fire.'

We decorated it with Mum's 1950s baubles, mainly gold and blue, and a set of ten hand-carved wooden soldiers dressed in red uniforms and wearing Foreign Legion hats, which looked like fezzes but with a veil down the back and a wide-rimmed peak. 'I can't remember where we got those from,' said Mum, holding up one of the models.

'Aunt Jess. She gave them to us when she cleared her house.'

'Oh,' she said, finally getting to the bottom of the sack, 'here it is.'

She pulled out a red velvet bag, unfolded it and held it up for examination. It had *Charlie* stitched across the front in white cotton. 'I can't have my little boy without his present bag.'

'Don't you think I'm getting a bit old for that, Mum?'

'Nonsense. Now put on that ABBA LP of mine and I'll fix us a drink.'

I went to the Ferguson cabinet record player, pulled *Arrival* out of the storage rack, a picture of the band in a helicopter on the front cover, and slid the record out of its sleeve. I dropped the black vinyl onto the turntable. The stylus arm landed with a crackle and the sound of "When I Kissed the Teacher" came through the single built-in speaker.

'Turn it up,' shouted Mum. 'I can hardly hear it.' She came back into the room, clutching two whisky tumblers and handed one to me.

'I don't know if I like whisky,' I said.

'Every man likes whisky. You're a big boy now.'

I took the glass and sipped. It burned the back of my throat as I swallowed.

'You'll get used to it,' she said. 'I've bought you something else today.' Her face shone with excitement. 'Come here,' she said.

I put down the glass and walked over to her.

She put my hand on her thigh. 'What can you feel?'

'Your leg. Do you want me to massage them?'

'Higher,' she said, shifting my hand position.

'It feels like a strap.'

'Sit down, Charlie. It's time to show you what real women wear.'

I sat, my mind racing, and she stood in front of me, slowly lifting her dress. Higher. Higher. And then. A stocking top, bare flesh, a suspender strap. 'What do you think?' she said, twirling in front of me, both legs on display.

'Gorgeous,' I said.

She placed my hand back on her leg, moving it from nylon to skin and back again. 'You're old enough to know about these now,' she said. 'I don't want some tart taking advantage. Come and dance with me.'

And we slow danced in front of the coal fire and Christmas tree to ABBA's "My Love, My Life". 'I love you, Charlie,' she whispered in my ear.

'I love you too, Mum.'

Mum and Boy

*

At ten years of age, I heard Mrs Poulton, a neighbour from up the block, say to Mum, 'It's a shame for him. Boys need their dads.'

'He's alright,' Mum said, 'aren't you, Charlie?' Mum told me later she was a nosy bitch and best ignored. I laughed, but I couldn't work out what Mrs Poulton was going on about. It seemed like a dumb thing to say. Having a dad would have meant sharing Mum and nothing could be worth that price. Anyway, standing out in a crowd suited us – 'It's not special if everyone's wearing the same thing, Charlie'. I never saw any dads that made me think other kids were better off. Beer gut losers pissing away money, chasing dreams at the bookies, wasting their way through life, giving out backhanders to their wives and offspring at the drop of a hat. Fuck that. Me and Mum were alright, and screw anyone who thought different.

I chased the man past Woolworths with its pick-and-mix counter; Smith's where Mum bought my football stickers and I started my collection of Crystal Gayle LPs; Littlewoods where my cousin worked as a supervisor – stuck up cow Mum called her. He moved quickly for a bloke I reckoned to be in his fifties. I wondered where Mum had gone, why she'd kept her date so brief. She seemed keen on him from what I saw and, as far as I knew, she had nothing else planned. But what did I know? I thought bingo was the main event of her day. Perhaps these liaisons were common, a string of men queuing round the block. Mum a slapper. I couldn't picture it.

He stopped, put his umbrella on the floor and tied one of his boot laces.

I juddered to a halt, conscious that, if I didn't, I'd be right next to him. Wasn't that the point? I hadn't given any thought to what I would say if I reached him. I knew what I wanted to do, what I needed to do, but that wouldn't be easy. How do you even go about doing something like that? It's one thing thinking, but when it comes to the crunch…

He started moving again. I followed him, trying to get a grip on my thoughts. Mum and a string of men. That didn't make sense. The only person she'd ever flirted with was me. Everyone else stayed away or she avoided them. Her motto, "Never tell anyone your business, Charlie", dictated the way we lived our lives. We barely knew the neighbours, hardly ever socialised, and neither of us had any friends. Loners, most people would say. Except we had each other. That was the point. Nothing came between us until… it couldn't be Mum. It had to be him. He'd taken advantage, preyed on her vulnerability, caught her in a moment of weakness. She'd never have betrayed me if he'd left her alone, stopped pick, pick, picking away at her. He'd probably had her in his sights for months, scheming and plotting, doing little favours. She'd fall for that. A gentleman. Like Trevor Howard. That's what had happened. He'd blinded her with his charade. And now he wanted to stroke his dirty fucking hands all the way up her thighs.

I quickened my pace.

*

A couple of years ago, Mum fetched her dressing-up box out on her birthday.

'Time to play, Charlie,' she called.

The box overflowed with old dresses and skirts, none of which she had the willpower to throw away. I pulled out a canary-yellow miniskirt. 'This one's like a belt,' I said.

'I wore that when I met your dad,' she said.

'How did you get into it?'

'With a squeeze. I couldn't fit one leg in there now. It did make my legs ache.'

I gave her a puzzled look.

'I couldn't sit down all night,' she said, laughing.

'I can see why Dad noticed you.'

'Turns out that's all he wanted. Put it on then.'

'I can't—'

'Yes, you can. You've got lovely legs. Let's have a look.'

'Mum—'

'Do it for me,' she said. 'It'll be nice to see it out the box.'

I hesitated before unzipping the skirt.

'You'll have to take your jeans off,' she said. 'That wouldn't be a good look.'

The skirt slipped easily up my bare legs and over my waist. I felt her eyes marking my every move. She zipped me up.

I posed, holding up my arms.

'Lovely,' she said, dropping to her knees in front of me and stroking the back of my calf. 'You've definitely inherited my legs.'

'You've got lovely legs, Mum.'

'There is just one problem, though. Your VPL.'

'My—'

'Those boxer shorts will have to come off, my darling.'

*

I stood behind him at a main road junction, just opposite Debenhams.

Other people waited, shuffling about, looking left, right, praying for a gap in the traffic. On one side of me, an old woman leaned on her shopping trolley, reading Graham Greene's *Travels With My Aunt*. She seemed engrossed in the book, which I admired because I needed to be totally at peace to read anything. No distractions. No movements. Even reading on a train or in a car jolted my concentration; taking my eye off the world for a second made me nauseous. On my other side, a little girl stared up at me, licking her ice cream. 'Sorry,' said the woman holding her hand. 'She's always doing that. We've told her not to.'

I smiled and looked again at the man. I expected him to be taller. He looked the same height as me, but from a distance, next to Mum, in his red Docs and cap, he seemed to tower above her. That felt odd because Mum stood at my height, and when we snuggled up on the settee to watch telly, we were exactly the same. But then I remembered she wasn't wearing her heels.

Me and Mum lying together. Her stroking my hair, kissing the top of my head.

The man and Mum. Him on top of her, greedily rolling up her skirt.

I wanted to grab him and spit "dirty bastard" into his face.

'Do you want a lick of my ice cream, mister?' The little girl with creamy lips.

'Come away,' said the woman, yanking her along the pavement.

I turned back to the man. He stared at me. Flinty blue eyes, exactly like mine. He faced the road again, stepped nearer the kerb. I edged forward.

Mum's face, his lips smothering her mouth, his hands... dirty bastard. Dirty bastard.

I had to... I shoved him hard.

Panic. Screaming.

'He pushed him.'

'He pushed him.'

I couldn't move, my legs frozen to the spot.

'Charlie,' said Mum, her eyes filled with tears. 'Charlie.'

*

And that's it. Dad dead and I never got a chance to say hello or goodbye. He stuck to the lorry for a screeching eternity, which meant I didn't have to face him. At least that's something.

I have no regrets. Him and Mum agreeing to meet up in Debenhams, next door to his block of flats, means he planned to screw her to his bed, chalk up a score on his board. I stopped him staining her, which must be a good thing. They'd been seeing each other for weeks after a chance meeting in the park. She hadn't known how to tell me, and now it's too late.

I worry about her. She needs me, but the doctors

think I'm better off here for a while. Maybe they're right. We need a break, but it's not over. Not by a long way. We love each other, and marriage isn't something you go into lightly.

Iris May

Drool dribbles over Mum's lips, her suck and rasp breathing reverberating around the house. She inhales, holds her breath and then exhales. I watch, hold my breath and wait. She starts again. Suck, blow, suck, blow. And then, nothing. I squeeze her hand. All the light in our house dulls to vanilla. It's over.

I flop on the settee and stare at her. She looks peaceful in her rocking chair, head facing the ceiling, eyes closed. Thank God. I don't want her staring at me. She's left the curtains open, never wanting to be hemmed in, which means I'm looking out at Dad's lawn, the one he grew from seed, and his rhubarb patch and his garage. Late evening shadows creep across the glass. The reflection of the room looms and makes me jump.

A fourteen-year-old boy in his school uniform, sitting opposite his dead mum.

I stretch my leg and tap the rockers, listen to the chair creak backwards and forwards, think of the hours Mum spent resting her eyes. The green Dralon seat has faded, and there's a rip in the fabric where some of the stuffing peeps out. A single sheet of blue notepaper lies in the centre of a coffee table, at its side a Mercedes bubble glass ashtray loaded with a stash of assorted colour tablets, purple, blue and white. The paper has a serrated edge where it's been torn from her pad by the telephone and is folded in half, my name written across its centre in her scrawly left-handed writing. The pills look like a jar of sweets waiting to be weighed into quarter-pound bags. "Little tonic drops" Mum called them. Next to the astray is a tumbler filled with water.

I make my head click and search. She's here. My comforter. Waiting for me. 'You knew it would happen,' she says.

'Not yet, though. I wanted more time.'

'She must have been desperate, Archie.'

'I know, but to just go—'

'She's left you a note.'

'I saw it.'

Crows screech from the garden. They've scuttled about in our loft for years, keeping me awake. Mum said Dad threatened to stuff newspaper in the soffit hole and leave them to starve. He never got round to it before he died. I'm glad. Familiarity settled Mum on her good days. Like the spider's web in the outside toilet; Dad's eucalyptus tree branches scratching against the back bedroom window when the wind blows; the loose floorboard on the landing creaking at the slightest tread; and the dripping tap in the kitchen sink. They've all been left. Mum named the spider, Harry. 'He's chosen to live with us for a reason, Archie.' Furniture, carpets, ornaments, all stuck in time. No new light shades, no pictures on the walls. Not quite Miss Havisham, but not far off.

    I pick up the note, unfold the paper and read.
    See you soon, Archie. I'll find Dad and wait for you.

*

Mum nursed Dad at home while the surgeons chased cancer around his body.

    He died lying next to her, and she sat on the bench opposite his grave every day for weeks until she heard him tell her to bugger off and raise the kid. That's when I became her little seven-year-old crutch. She kept me off school for months with a mystery kidney infection. Me in my pyjamas, lying on the settee, making up cowboy and Indian games, talking to my teddies. Dr Dwyer visited every other day in his worsted wool suit, stethoscope hanging round his neck. Shortly afterwards, my fits started. I could bring those on by lying in her bed, gently rubbing the sheets between my thumb and forefinger, over and over until the smell of burning filled my nostrils and I drifted off into another world.

A sickly child to keep indoors. That's what she wanted, and that's what she got.

We'd sit in front of the coal fire watching telly, me holding her when she cried, staring into the embers, mesmerised by the yellow and blue dancing flames, the white heat spot, imagining a world of fairy-fire-folk inhabiting a burning universe; our cosy winter nights together, rain and wind locked out, nothing but each other. No lights, no telly, fire stacked and roaring up the chimney; us lying on the carpet, Mum touching my cheeks, making me move back from the grate, telling me I'd burn my face. A safe existence. Magical, but it felt wrong when the outside world interrupted. Like the time last year when Tomo and Colin Taylor, friends from school, stuck their faces against the window and saw us curled up together in this room. That's when the name-calling started. "Mummy's boy". It made my skin crawl, got me into lots of fights.

I look across at her, touch her hand. She's still warm.

A shadow in the corner of the room makes me jump. 'You have to call someone.'

'I can't. They'll take her away.'

'But she's dead, Archie. It's over.'

This house. Mum's domain. I want to stay, carry on breathing in the spaces we shared, wandering the places she used to be. The landing where I laid my Scalextric track; the spare room with my dartboard hanging on the back of the door; the garden where I kicked my Casey ball against Dad's white gates. She rarely left home, and now she's gone.

I tap my foot on the rockers again and stroke the arm of her chair. A shiver drips down my back.

*

I can't stop looking at the note and the pills.

See you soon, Archie. I'll find Dad and wait for you.

It's always been me and Mum. Dad dying left a wormhole, which we filled with each other. She made me her plus-one at family weddings, giving me a basin haircut and dressing me in a navy-blue, double-breasted blazer and chocolate-brown trousers. And now I'm alone. I'm not sure what'll happen. This house. Her stuff. A dressing table mirror with her image ingrained in the glass, brushing the knots out of her long, black hair; her bed with its mustard-coloured candlewick bedspread, its steel frame bolted together with a special spanner that hangs from one of the posts; her oak-veneered sideboard with Dad's pink dish as its centrepiece. It'll all have to be sorted.

The Seiko clock ticks on the wall behind me. It's been around forever, but I don't think she told me who bought it. I've never seen her change the battery.

It just *tick, tick, ticks* away, sounding louder at night. Time seems to move more urgently when it's dark.

'What will happen to me?'

'You're a child, Archie. They'll sort you out.'

'I could just leave her.'

'I don't understand.'

'Carry on like before.'

'That's crazy.'

It sounds bonkers, but possible. I could cover her with a green wool blanket, cash her widow's pension, live around her. The smell would subside as she became part of the rocker. I take a deep breath, tell myself to get my sensible head fixed. The council will step in, bury Mum, find me somewhere to go. But I can look after myself. I know that. I've been doing her washing, cooking, watching her mood slaloming downhill for the last year. 'We don't need anyone, Archie.' Last May, she asked me to plant irises in the front garden, a clump of them by the door. They're blooming at the moment.

She liked irises and, of course, that was her name. Iris May.

*

Her body rocks away in front of me.

Colour has drained from her face and lips, leaving her waxen and chalky. I want to touch her skin again, but I'm frightened of how it might feel. The thought of cold and clammy makes me nauseous. Lank hair sticks to her scalp, the long brush strokes that made it so shiny abandoned as depression dragged her mood into a pit. She's wearing a white Aran wool cardigan she knitted herself, food stains clinging to the braids, and the shift dress she's lived in for the last few months. Her hard-skin feet are rammed into sloppy slippers; her bare legs blemished by the varicose veins she came to detest. False teeth poke out of her mouth, ill fitted because of the weight she's lost. Dad said it made sense to have her teeth out when she fell pregnant. 'No point in paying later when you can get them sorted for free now.' It makes me sad to see them stained. She soaked them religiously every night in a glass at the side of her bed.

I turn my head away. Death has taken her now, but she could have blossomed, been so much more than she became. Everything seemed to get in her way. Granddad wouldn't let her go to grammar school, even though she passed the exams, and then Dad wanted a housewife, which trapped her again. She liked looking after him, baking bread and butter puddings, going on holiday to Dawlish Warren, her favourite place in the world. All the pictures show me needing a wee, holding myself, looking up at Mum. The only photo I've seen of just me and Dad is me crying, holding Dad's cardigan pocket, waiting for Mum to put the camera down and have me back. Dad looks ill. I'm about four or five, and he was dead by the time I reached seven. Mum never said if he knew me when he was well. I guess I'll never know now.

I'd love to have seen her happy. Courting her handsome sailor, her wedding day, having me so late in life. She met Dad in Granddad's pub when he was home on leave from the merchant navy. A chance meeting. Him in the wrong pub, having misremembered the name his mate, Tommy Wood, told him, and her covering for half an hour as a favour while Granddad had his tea.

Granny died before Mum's first birthday. She became a daddy's girl, and I became a mummy's boy.

Mum rolled with laughter, her eyes shining, face crinkling, when she told her stories of Granddad playing the piano and leading the sing-song in his pub, his trilby hat worn at a jaunty angle. She has a photo of him swanning arm in arm along Blackpool pier with his new wife, his ex-housekeeper whom he married a year after Granny died. His children asked him what he was leaving in his will, and he said, 'The world. Enjoy it. I have.' He died a couple of weeks before I was born – something else that happened in May.

'You both lost parents when you were children.'

My comforter, interrupting my thoughts.

'Granddad swamped her. She became overprotected.'

'Is that a bad thing?'

'It is when it's taken away.'

'But she had brothers and sisters.'

'They were nothing like her.'

All of Mum's siblings were high volume, centre stage, but she was shy, the baby of the family. Her two sisters, Doris and Theresa, swore and drank like troopers. I never heard Mum say more than "bloody", and a glass of advocaat was her very occasional tipple. When I was eight, we went to Uncle Norman's twenty-fifth wedding anniversary party. Doris grabbed me as I walked past her armchair and kissed me with puckered lips covered in cherry-red lipstick. Mum said she was "sozzled". Theresa used to shout, 'Get the pissing kettle on, Iris,' when she walked through our back door unannounced. My favourite was Uncle Arthur, the eldest brother, named after Granddad. I might have turned him into an all-action hero, the kind I used to read about in the adventure stories Mum bought me. He used to sneak me bottles of shandy and packets of chicken crisps at the Gunners Club in Bloxwich. The other club was Colebatch's. I'd watch Frankenstein and Dracula films on a Friday night with my cousin, Jane. I'd be about ten or eleven, and me and Mum would walk there mostly.

'Sounds like fun, Archie.'

'It made her cry. Reminded her of Dad not being there.'

'But you—'

'She was alone. That's all she could think of for the last year. Even I wasn't enough.'

I miss Uncle Arthur and his big continental car with leather upholstery and walnut veneer. Ex-army, still served in the territorials. Mum has a picture of him looking like a young Errol Flynn, with a trace of a moustache. He used to wipe the seat with a white handkerchief before he sat down in Granddad's pub. 'Clean enough for you now, Arthur.' His first wife left him while he was serving abroad, emptied their house of his possessions. His second wife, Peggy, had a stroke, which left her bedbound. He cared for her single-handedly, refusing all offers of help, his only break a swift half in a local pub. He came to our house after Peggy died, and Mum cooked him Sunday lunch. And then he met someone else, moved to Birmingham to be with his new woman but still kept his bolthole flat in Bloxwich. He died in May last year. I can't remember if Mum went to the funeral.

Mum a Taurus baby. Me a Gemini. Both born in May. And now it's May again and Mum is dead.

I pick up the note.

*

I should get out of this room, stop tapping the rockers with my foot. It's properly dark outside, and stars have plopped into the sky.

My favourite place in our house is lying in bed, mesmerised by the changing scene as it rolls past the window. A top-of-the-hill view means a clear horizon, like a framed painting, ever altering according to season and time of day, shape shifting with colours bleeding into each other from the painter's palette. Vivid sunsets morph into pastel, calm evenings; misty Shropshire mornings become booming thundercloud vistas, all transformed by moon size, magnitude of stars, brightness of sun, opaqueness of cloud cover. It drags me away, takes my head on a magical journey. When Dad died, I stood in the garden, a little boy looking up at the universe, talking to him, imagining his new home in the clouds.

Mum used to stand with me. I wonder where she is now, if she can see me, what she'd say.

'She can see you, Archie.'

'How do you know?'

'She's watching you right now.'

I read the note again, the idea of Mum with her eyes on me fills my head. She must have given the tablets a lot of thought, stashed them for months to create this hoard. She seemed to take them when I reminded her. Perhaps she pouched them, pretended to swallow, but there's too many here for that to have been enough. I wonder if they're all hers. Maybe some of them are Dad's. I don't remember her getting rid of his pills.

See you soon, Archie. I'll find Dad and wait for you.

It makes sense. Living on my own in God knows where, with God knows who for company. Fourteen years old. Who'll want me now? She knows I'll do it. I've always done as I'm told. 'You're a good boy, Archie. Do what Mummy tells you.'

'They'll sort you out, Archie. You need to phone someone.'

'But that's not the life I want.'

'You're a child—'

'Stop saying that.'

Mum will be waiting. She never coped with being alone. That's why she went for a bitter lemon and a game of bingo with George, a security guard who wore a trilby hat and drove a three-wheel Reliant Robin that got sniggered at in the street. He drove us to the club one night, and we leant towards him as he turned a corner, which made Mum laugh. He didn't hang around long. Turned out he was married, but I guess having a little boy in tow didn't help her chances. 'We're okay, Archie. Just you and me.' She said we were like Fred and Ginger, but getting her out of bed became harder and harder. She wanted so badly for us to work. To be perfect.

'No family is perfect, Archie.'

'In Mum's head it had to be. To make up for Dad dying.'

'I don't understand.'

'He told her to keep me safe, how to rear me.'

'He gave her instructions?'

'Yeah, and she tried to follow them.'

'But—'

'I know. She gave up in the end.'

I reach for the water.

*

My hand starts to shake as I raise the tumbler to my lips.

'What are you doing?'

'Taking a drink.'

'You can't do as she asks, Archie. Not this time.'

I fix my eyes on Joey's empty bird cage – Mum's budgie who died last summer. I had to get rid of his body by putting him in a sugar bag and dropping him in the bin. For fourteen years he glared through the bars and gnawed on his cuttlefish. He rarely got cleaned out. 'Joey's got his wellies on,' Mum used to say. On a good day, Mum made kissing noises through his bars and whispered, 'Who's a pretty boy?' He'd race along his perch towards her, snapping with his beak. She'd pull her head back, startled. 'That bird hates me,' she'd say. She let him fly around the lounge, but he attacked her like he'd been planning his assault for weeks. He never got out again. She left the cage hanging from the ceiling.

The telephone rings. I look at the Seiko clock. No one phones the house, especially this time of night. Mum ignores it, and I never have a reason to pick up.

The answer machine clicks in. 'Iris. Are you there, Iris? I got your message. I've just got back from bingo. I'm worried sick. Look at the time. Where's that lad of yours? Phone me back. God, I hate talking to these things.' The line goes dead.

Aunt Lil. Nearly seventy. The last of the aunty-uncle brigade. Mum never liked her, but they had weekly coffee stops in Littlewoods' café, mainly because they were the only ones still breathing. They haven't met for a couple of years, but the last time I heard Mum really chuckle was when Aunt Lil told her one of my cousins had turned out a lesbian – Lil had to mouth the word in case she became infected.

I take a sip of water. 'You called Lil,' I say, tapping the rocking chair again.

'You'll have to tell someone now, Archie.'

Mum's left arm falls off her lap and swings gently with the rock. Backwards and forwards; backwards and forwards. I reach over and rest it on her knees, stopping the chair in the process. The jolt causes Mum's head to jar sideways and makes her burb. 'Jesus,' I say, falling into the settee, spilling the water over my school blazer. I reach out and touch her arm. It feels like a shank of lamb straight out of the fridge.

'She's dead.'

'I know.'

The phone rings again.

*

'Hello. Hello.'

'Aunt Lil.'

'Archie. Thank God. I'm trying to get your mum.'

'She's in bed.'

'Is she okay?'

'She's had a good day today.'

'But she left this awful message, Archie. Saying goodbye.'

'When?'

'This afternoon. I've been at Margaret's for tea and then bingo. I shouldn't have gone. She overcooked the gammon and I didn't win. I never win these days. Your mum sounded… but she's alright?'

'You know what she's like.'

'I've been worried sick. I phoned earlier—'

'We're in bed, Aunt Lil. Have you seen the time?'

'Tell her to call me, Archie. Will you do that?'

'I'll tell her tomorrow.'

'You're a good boy, looking after your mum.'

'Goodnight, Aunt Lil.'

'Goodnight, sweetheart. Sleep tight. Don't let the bed bugs bite.'

*

I refill the tumbler from the kitchen tap, walk back into the lounge and place it on the coffee table next to the ashtray full of pills. The only light in the room comes from a purple shaded standard lamp sitting behind the television. A chill fills the air; goosebumps prickle my arms.

I close the curtains and sit on the settee.

Aunt Lil. The last of Mum's family apart from me.

Mum wanted us to be like royalty, imagined them as perfect, and she gave me an image of *2 Point 4 Children* happiness, a house full of love straight out of Enid Blyton. I wonder where that hope came from. I'm guessing losing her mum at a young age, Granddad remarrying, pushing her into a fantasy world, one that infected me.

We had some of it for a while, but Dad dying snatched it away.

'All families are different, Archie.'

'I guess.'

'You know that's right. Look at this street.'

It's true. Mrs Hedges, next door, lives on her own. She has one arm, and it fascinates me that she can still peg her washing out. Her daughters, Molly and Jessica, bring the grandkids round every weekend, and they play Olympics in the garden. On the other side, the Rayboulds with fifteen children. 'First up, best dressed in that house,' said Mum. A couple of doors down, the Reeces. A bit stuck up, outsiders in the street. A gang of lads threw Mr Reece in the canal because they didn't like his hat. Me and Mum laughed about that. And then, across the road, the Tolleys. Their dad chases his kids round the block, threatening to lamp them. 'You'd need to be a fast runner in that house,' said Mum.

I tap Mum's rocker again.

'You lied to Lil, Archie.'

'What else could I do?'

'Tell her. Tell someone.'

My comforter's voice sounds urgent, but the thought of losing my home, of Mum not being in my life, makes my brain scream. I imagine going to school, looking after myself, using Mum's money. Nothing changes. No one would notice. The only difference is Mum dead in her chair and things taking their natural course. She wouldn't need me. I could push her into a corner, surround her with scented candles…

'You can't exist that way, Archie.'

'Why not?'

'People don't. It would come out eventually.'

'Maybe.'

I stand up, walk over to the window, open the curtains.

Beyond the reflection of the room, a blackout has dropped over the garden, but I know Dad's seed-grown lawn is in front of me. It wouldn't take much digging. Wrap her in a sheet and plant her near the eucalyptus tree. She'd like that. Still here, in sight of the house, close enough for me to tend her grave without raising suspicion. I could cover her over with turf, plant more irises above her. And then get on with my life. Finish school, get a job, get married, have a family.

'Archie.'

I close the curtains and sit back down on the settee. Mum has stopped rocking. I look at the note, the pills, the tumbler of water.

'Please don't, Archie.'

'I have to do what Mummy tells me.'

*

It could have been worse. She could have left me a gun or a rope. At least pills are easy. I'm glad she's given me water and not whisky.

All the films choose whisky, but that increases the risk of throwing up and dragging the drugs out of my system before the deed is done. The only thing missing is a sprinkling of sugar to help them slip down without gagging. It's quite a stash. I recognise her tranquilisers and sleeping pills. Speed is important, get enough inside before I pass out. Handfuls at a time is probably best. I'll take gulps of water. I don't want the misery of failure.

I lean forward, pick up the tumbler, dip my hand in the ashtray.

'You're really going to do this, Archie?'

'What choice do I have?'

'To think about you, your life.'

'There isn't a me. There never has been.'

'You've got a chance to change things. A way out.'

I look at Mum. Her head slumps forward, her top set of dentures land in her lap. The chair is perfectly still. The only noise in the room is the *tick, tick, tick* of the Seiko clock.

I take my hand out of the ashtray and touch my face. Tears drip down my cheeks.

Talking Heads

A streak of bathroom light illuminates my bedroom through the glass partition over the doorway. I flinch as Mum's toothbrush clatters into its mug and the basin tap stops running. I want to shout out, 'Leave the light on, Mum. Leave the light on,' but I'm fifteen, almost a man. A click brings darkness. I stare into air bubbles, waiting for faces to meld into existence. I know they're here, lurking, biding their time. 'Leave me alone,' I whisper, pulling the duvet under my chin.

A movement by the single wardrobe.

Floaters cut across my vision, blurring everything, and then, a man's head, goatee beard, chipped front tooth, a scar of a cross pulsating in the centre of his forehead. 'She's a slag,' he says. 'Can't keep her knickers on, that one.' He hovers at the foot of my bed, a rictus on his face.

'No,' I say, trying not to raise my voice, not wanting to disturb Mum.

'It's true,' says another head from over by the tallboy. A woman, red hair, button nose, piercing blue eyes. She's wearing a black fedora, which she lifts in greeting when I look over. 'Always at it,' she says, zooming around the big light.

'No. No. No.'

Two more heads race from the corners. A Tom Selleck lookalike with a pink cravat tied loosely under his dimpled chin; a chalk-faced woman with spiky, blonde hair and a Union Jack stud pierced through her nose. Fedora flies over to make up a foursome. They bob up and down and chant in unison. 'Tart. Slag. Tart. Slag.'

I scream. My door opens. The heads spin towards the light and evaporate.

'Alfie… what on earth…' Mum races over and switches on my bedside lamp.

'They're here, Mum,' I say, grabbing her arm. 'They're here.'

'You're burning up,' she says, touching my brow. 'Let me fetch a flannel.'

'Don't leave me. They're watching, saying things.'

'There's no one here, sweetheart. You've had a bad dream. I'll just be a minute.'

I let her go.

'Slag. Slag. Slag.' Whispers from the skirting boards fill the room. 'Slag. Slag. Slag.'

*

Mum's knock-off turned up a few days before my fifteenth birthday. He plonked himself on the settee and watched *Corrie*.

She's done it before, six months ago, but that bloke, Tony, buggered off after a couple of weeks, saying she suffocated him, and he needed space. His ice-cream van still stops in our street most Sundays, the tinny jingle of "Teddy Bears' Picnic" announcing his presence like a clarion call. Magnums for pudding every night is the thing I remember about Tony. Mum never bought them after he left, went back to tinned peaches with Carnation milk. Healthier, but not the same.

Her new guy, Gary, works in a carpet factory, so I'm guessing we'll have the floors re-covered soon. Mum says she met him at a disco in The Knave pub, that he has kind eyes and a nice smile, does a bit of cash-in-hand behind the bar, which means free gin night when he's on shift. 'A bit of company,' she says.

The heads mutter a different story:

'Skirt riding up her thighs.'

'Reliving her teenage vamp years.'

'Rubbing up and down to the purr of Roxy Music.'

'Dirty cow. Lassoing freshers, bits of kids, making their hormones explode.'

Mum and Gary. They're up in the bedroom now.

I stare at Dad, who's sitting in his armchair

opposite me. We're watching *Only Fools and Horses*, but the noise of bouncing springs through the ceiling makes me want to retch. 'Doesn't it bother you?' I say.

'She'll be done in a minute,' he says, fixing his gaze on Del Boy and Trigger pratting about as yuppies in a wine bar.

Mum's moans trickle through the lightshade. I melt into my chair, my face flush with embarrassment.

*

When Dad was my age, Mum had just been born. They met thirty-six years later. His first proper girlfriend.

Here's Dad's story. First half, before Mum, Granny Margaret making salmon and cucumber sandwiches and flasks of coffee for their trips out, ticking off railway stations and train engines, keeping him under her skirts, hiding him from the world. His perfect day, a trip to London in his forties, looking through the gates of Buckingham Palace, staring at the balcony, imagining generation after generation of royals waving at the nation.

Second half, Granny dies, and he meets Mum on his only visit to a nightclub. He sits on a bar stool, sipping a cola, watching the dance floor. Blondie's "Dreaming" starts up and Mum, a petite blonde, strides over, barefoot, in her Indian Squaw dress, kisses him on the lips and demands a dance.

Dad's life in his own words. 'My rescue angel,' he'd say, stroking Mum's hand. 'Why did you choose me?'

'You had "marry me" eyes,' she'd reply.

'She seduced him,' whispers Fedora. 'Stuck her claws in and wouldn't let go.'

I can see that now. Vulnerable, alone. Three months after their first dance, Mum got him to tie the knot, and I arrived eighteen months later. He must have thought nirvana awaited, but she hooked him and Granny's house before trapping him with a kid. It's taken me months to see what's real, watching him shrivel to a husk as she plays with her "friends". 'Who's your mum fucking these days, tart boy?' That's what the heads say when they know she's been tramping through town.

And now Gary's here and he's shagging Mum through the lounge ceiling.

Stop. Stop. Stop. That's me screaming inside my head.

'She can't stop. That's what she does.' Goatee man leers at me from the edge of the curtain rail.

Dad looks over and we smile at each other.

Mum lets out a high-pitched moan.

*

It goes quiet. Footsteps drop on the bedroom floor. Someone pads across the landing. The toilet flushes.

'Told you they wouldn't be long,' says Dad.

'What does he know?' says Fedora, her red hair trailing along the top of the telly.

She's right. Naïve Dad. No life sense. A bit like me. Chip off the old block. We spend a lot of time watching telly and working on his model railway collection, which he's set up across the whole floor space in the loft. He disappears upstairs, not saying a word, and I join him, knowing he'll put me in charge of signals, which always makes me smile. He sleeps in my room, climbed in the spare bed next to me one night and stayed there, holding my hand when Mum turns out the light.

I'm glad. Sleeping on my own isn't good, especially with the things that live in the dark.

Mum doesn't get it. Not that I've told her. She's too busy lying on her back, moaning.

The springs start up again. I clench my fists.

*

It hasn't always been this way.

Me, Mum and Dad, a proper family, going to the arboretum for a picnic; Dad whistling a Perry Como song, "Fly Me to the Moon", as he spreads a blanket next to a stream. Mum busying herself, batting away wasps, tutting as she sets out paper plates, cheese and onion sandwiches, a homemade Victoria sponge, alongside sausage rolls and pasties bought from Eley's pastry shop in Ironbridge. After we've eaten, Mum sunbathes in her cerise bikini, listening to Gary Davies on Radio 1, while me and Dad play football with a Casey bought from a second-hand shop in town. Mum shades her eyes and shouts at him, 'Run faster. You're like a little old man.' He goes over, tickles her, and they roll on the blanket laughing while I do keepie-uppies with the ball.

A nice memory, but something happened. Grown-up stuff. Dad went away and then came back to sleep with me. I'm scared to tell Mum, not sure what she might say. She seemed upset when he left. I listened at her bedroom door, heard her sobbing. She spoiled me for a while, bought me loads of new clothes. Melancholy dropped like a blackout curtain, but my floating heads appeared, started talking to me, which helped it all make sense.

And then Mum brought Tony home… and now Gary.

'She'd stop if you asked her,' I say.

'She needs comfort,' says Dad, not taking his eyes off the telly. 'We all do.'

I want to shake him to life.

Del Boy falls through a gap in the bar.

*

Dad shushes me down when the talking heads make me cry, asks me to close my eyes and wish them gone. He cuddles me close. I smell a leathery tang from his garden day sweat, which is odd because he hasn't been out there since he came back. His acer and yew trees are taking over, making me cross because he kept them beautifully trimmed and shaped. Mum threatened to get a gardener, but she hasn't bothered so far. Maybe she should have vetted Gary and Tony before she danced with them. We don't really need carpets, and we could have lived without Magnums.

'That's not what she needs,' whispers Tom Selleck, bobbing on the arm of my chair. He touches his cravat and winks. 'You know what she wants. Don't you?'

I stand up and walk into the kitchen. The heads follow me, but Dad stays glued to the telly, watching Rodney get soaked as he walks home in a downpour wearing Cassandra's raincoat.

Dad laughs.

Mum groans.

Do something, I scream inside my head. *Do something.*

*

I run the tap, fill a tumbler with water and lean against the cooker. Mum baked a lot before Dad left. Bread and butter puddings were her favourite and mine. She took up knitting for a while but gave it up when the purple jumper she clicked together for Dad stretched in the wash, arms trailing on the floor when she pegged it on the line. She broke her needles in front of us. Dad laughed and said, 'You can't be good at everything.' Mum kissed him and they went shopping.

And then he went away.

'He's back now.'

'She should be ashamed of herself, carrying on in front of him.'

Fedora and Spiky-Blonde bounce on the worksurface, talking to each other. 'Found herself a new hobby.'

'Puts more of a smile on her face than playing with wool.'

Shut up. Shut up.

I open the knife drawer and inspect them one by one.

*

They lost me when I was seven.

We were strolling along a coastal path in Cornwall, Dad and Mum in front, holding hands. Mum said I couldn't have another ice cream, which put me with a mardy face, slouching behind them. Dad said to ignore me, and they turned a corner, dropping out of sight. I left the path, into the undergrowth, and hid behind a tree. Mum came back. 'Alfie. Alfie.' And then Dad. 'It's your fault,' said Mum as they crashed through the brambles.

'How do you work that out?' said Dad.

'You've upset him.'

'You're the one that said he couldn't have an ice cream.'

I got bored and cried out, 'You've gone and left me and I'm only little.'

Mum hugged me and made Dad walk back to the caravan park to fetch a 99.

'A spoiled brat.'

'No wonder she wants a bit of me time.'

Fedora and Goatee muttering from behind me.

I squeeze a steak knife into the palm of my left hand. Blood drips through my fingers and onto the green porcelain floor tiles.

'He needs to stop her,' says Fedora.

'Before it's too late,' says Goatee.

I walk down the hallway.

*

There's no sound coming from the lounge as I stand at the bottom of the stairs. Dad must have switched off the telly. I wonder if he's in the loft, setting up his new Hornby. Maybe I'll join him, help sort out a new piece of track to create a sharper bend underneath the cobwebbed eaves. We've been wanting to do that for ages, get more speed up as the train whizzes across the lines.

I look up at the landing. A picture of Mum and Dad on their wedding day, him looking at her like she's dropped into his lap from a Hollywood film. Underneath the picture, on an oak corner unit, a pink glass dish with a dancing nymph statue Dad bought Mum as a Christmas present two years ago. She shines it up every day, wishes the statue would come to life and teach her to waltz. 'Like Fred and Ginger,' she says.

I squeeze the knife, wincing as the blade cuts my flesh.

A noise from Mum's bedroom.

The heads line up on ascending steps in front of me.

'She's starting again.'

'It's never going to stop.'

'Slag. Slag. Slag.'

'You have to do something.'

Shut up. Shut up.

More blood rolls down my wrist, this time plopping onto the carpet.

I climb the stairs.

*

What Mum doesn't know is there's a slight chip in the base of her pink dish. I caught it with the loft ladder last summer, but it was a perfect break and I managed to glue it back in place with Bostick. I touch the spot. I could never tell her. She'd be too upset.

'She knows, Alfie.' Dad puts his hand on my shoulder. He's standing in front of Mum's bedroom door.

'What do you mean?'

'She found it the day after you stuck it in place.'

'She'd have said…'

'No, she wouldn't. You know she wouldn't.' He nods towards the knife. 'What are you going to do with that?'

'Stop her,' says Fedora.

'She's a tart,' says Spiky-Blonde.

Dad shakes his head and turns me back towards the stairs. We sit side by side on the top step. 'None of this is real, Alfie,' he says.

The four heads perch along the banister, grinning at me.

'I don't understand,' I say. 'How can you let her…'

'I don't, and she doesn't. You know that.'

'She has other men, Dad.'

'Two in eighteen months, and they've barely been in the house.'

'But you're still here…'

'Only for you, Alfie. I'm only here for you.'

I drop the knife. The heads have gone.

A key turns in the front door. 'Alfie,' shouts Mum, 'I'm back. Marks had run out of fondant fancies, so I've bought eclairs. Gary's given me a lift so I've said he can come in for a coffee... what's all this on the floor? Alfie. Where are you?'

'Go and have your cake,' says Dad. 'I'll be up in the loft when you're ready.'

Final Thoughts

Philip Larkin's poem, "This Be The Verse", opens with the line, "They fuck you up, your mum and dad", and describes how parents inflict their flaws on their children, who in turn inhabit them and pass them on to their children. On and on the fractures and emotional failings go, dripping through the generations. Larkin's advice is to get out early and not have any kids. It's all tongue in cheek, but it strikes a chord because it has a basis in reality.

My mum has been dead for nearly twenty years now, and it still catches in my throat when I think of her no longer in the world, not on the end of a telephone, not sitting in her flat waiting patiently for her children and grandchildren to grace her life with their presence. That sounds harsh, but it's what she did, and we didn't do it often enough. We didn't appreciate what we had, what she represented, until she was no longer there. Well, we know now. She anchored the family, carried the stories, gave us a place of refuge when life blew up in our face, which, in my case, it so often did. I wish I could see her again, spend time listening to her lovely chuckle and bask in the joy of her unconditional love. No one has ever looked at me like my mum. No judgement. No assumptions. No prejudice. That's quite a thing and a gap that can never be filled.

I miss you, Mum. I hope you found Dad.

Thank you to Dr Alison Taft for her advice and guidance on an early draft of these stories.

All of these stories were crafted on a writing retreat in Scarborough in July 2023. Writing by the sea is something I can highly recommend.

About the Author

Stephen Brotherton grew up in the West Midlands and now lives in Shropshire. A social worker for nearly thirty years, he currently works for the NHS, and is a member of the Bridgnorth Writers' Group. Mum and Boy is his second short-story collection.